Albert and the Garden of Doom

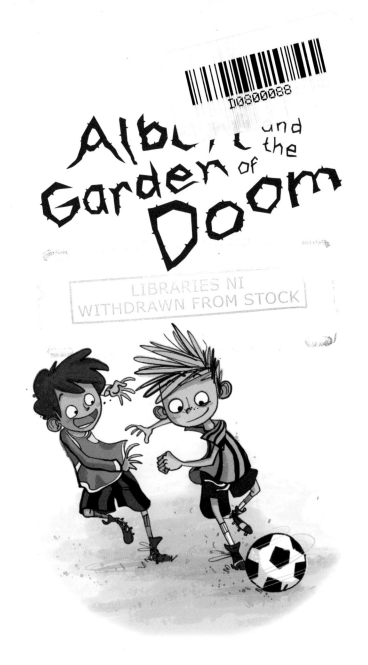

Albert and the Garden of Doom

Phil Earle

Illustrated by Jamie Littler

Orion
Children's Books

First published in Great Britain in 2015
by Orion Children's Books
an imprint of Hachette
Children's Group,
a division of Hodder and Stoughton Ltd.
Carmelite House
50 Victoria Embankment
London EC4Y 0DZ
An Hachette UK company

1 3 5 7 9 10 8 6 4 2

Text © Phil Earle 2015
Illustrations © Jamie Littler 2015

The right of Phil Earle and Jamie Littler to be identified
as author and illustrator of this work has been asserted.

A catalogue record for this book is available
from the British Library.

ISBN 978 1 4440 1358 0

Printed and bound in China

www.orionchildrensbooks.co.uk

*For my son, Albie, who has
the greatest left foot in the world.
And for our lovely neighbours,
Bob and Jamie, who always
throw our balls back. – P.E.*

*For Auntie Tricia, for always
being a supporter! – J.L.*

Contents

Chapter One

Albert (Albie to his friends) LOVED football.

Morning or night, awake or asleep, he thought of nothing else.

Albie loved spending all day in his garden, even if it was raining. He practised his dribbling and pretended he was playing in the Cup Final in front of ninety thousand fans.

"Here comes Albie," he'd chant. "He goes past two defenders, sees the keeper off his line and shoots GOOOOAAALLL!"

Albie never got bored of scoring goals.

He only stopped when the worst thing possible happened…

...when he kicked his ball into the
GARDEN OF DOOM!

Chapter Two

Albie wasn't scared of much (apart from maths lessons and sprouts), but the Garden of Doom made him shake in his football boots.

Normal gardens have lawns and flowers (and football pitches), but the Garden of Doom didn't have any of those things. It was a jungle of weeds so tall they looked like monsters from a scary movie.

Albie had lost count of how many balls he'd kicked over there, but his moneybox was always empty as a result.

You see, Albie never went to find his lost balls, because the garden belonged to someone even scarier than the weeds – Mr Creaky.

Mr Creaky had only lived next door for a short while, but in that time the garden had gone crazy.

Albie had never seen or spoken to Mr Creaky, because his neighbour NEVER went outside. Somehow though, the name 'Creaky' seemed right.

Albie thought he could sense
the old man watching him, though
when he looked up at the window,
it was always empty.

Albie tried to talk to Mum about it.

"What's his real name?" he asked.

"Who?" asked Mum.

"Mr Creaky next door."

Mum almost choked on her chips.

"Don't call him that!" Mum whispered. "He's an old man and he's all on his own. Anyway, why don't you ask him yourself? Your footballs are always flying over there and ruining his garden."

Albie laughed. It would take
a bomb to flatten those weeds,
and he didn't want to find out Mr
Creaky's real name. Not if it meant
talking to him.

Chapter Three

Next afternoon, while Albie was playing in the World Cup Final with his friend, Errol, disaster struck.

England was beating Brazil 19 – 18, when Albie's shot hit the bar and spun over the fence into the Garden of Doom!

'NOOOOOOOO!' Albie yelled.

It wasn't even his ball. It was
Errol's. Albie had kicked his last one
over yesterday when he beat a team
of aliens 100 – nil.

"I'll get it," said Errol,

"WAIT!" Albie yelled again.

"Be careful! Mr Creaky lives there!"

"Who?"

Albie explained.

"Maybe," said Errol, "He's not an old man at all! Maybe he's a retired jewel thief!"

Albie liked Errol's thinking. "Maybe he's hidden all the booty in the garden and covered it with weeds to confuse the police," he said.

Errol nodded. "And maybe, hidden in the weeds, there are robot cockroaches, designed to attack anyone who sets foot in the garden."

On they went, making up more and more stories, until the sun started to set behind the towering weeds.

"So, are you going to get your
ball or not?" Albie asked Errol. He
might have been scared, but he still
wanted to finish his game.

Errol looked at his watch. "Er …
actually, it's teatime."

And he ran towards the gate.

Albie sat on the grass and scowled at the Garden of Doom. His game was ruined – **AGAIN!**

Chapter Four

The next day brought a new match, and another friend, Oscar, who had brought his ball with him.

Albie was racing towards victory, when his left foot shot broke the net, before soaring into the Garden of Doom.

Albie wanted to scream.

Oscar did. **"MY BALL!**
It's brand new," he cried, running
towards the fence.

Albie pulled him back.

"Don't! Mr Creaky lives there,"
he said.

"Mr who?"

Albie told him.

"Maybe," said Oscar, "he's not an old man at all. Maybe he's a ghost!"

Albie liked Oscar's thinking. "Maybe he lived there hundreds of years ago and..."

"Maybe there are ghost dogs patrolling the garden, waiting for someone to climb the fence," said Oscar.

"So, are you going to get the ball or not?" Albie asked. He might have been scared, but he still wanted to finish his game.

"Er… I've just remembered, I've got karate class, bye!" And he ran towards the gate.

Albie was more fed up than ever. Mum had banned him from buying ANY more balls. What was he supposed to do now?

Just who was Mr Creaky really?
Was he a powerful wizard in
disguise?

Or a secret
agent hiding
from the
bad guys?

Or an alien, sent to Earth to steal a child who was REALLY good at football?

Albie didn't know, but enough was enough. He wanted his footballs back.

Chapter Five

Next day, Albie, Oscar and Errol stood in the shadows by the garden fence.

Albie was wearing a woolly hat.
Oscar had dark paint covering his
cheeks. Errol had his mum's tights
pulled over his face.

"We're not robbing a bank!"
Albie said, sighing.

Errol shrugged. "What's the plan?"
he asked.

"We sneak in, grab the balls and
get out!" said Albie bravely, though
inside he was shaking.

"What about the weeds?" asked
Oscar.

Albie took Dad's garden shears
out from behind his back.

"What about us?" said Errol.

Albie gave them a pair of blunt scissors and some nail clippers.

"It was all I could find," he said.

Errol and Oscar didn't look happy. In fact, they looked ready to go home, so Albie quickly promised them half of his secret supply of chocolate. (Which didn't actually exist. But sssshhhh! Don't tell them!)

47

A minute later, all three of them were over the fence and standing in the middle of the Garden of Doom.

Albie hacked at the weeds with his shears, Errol waved the scissors in the air like a mad hairdresser. Oscar got the clippers out of his pocket and thought about trimming his nails until…

"My ball!" shouted Albie. "There, there, there, there and there!" There were balls EVERYWHERE. Some of them so flat and covered in moss, it looked as if they had been there for years!

Albie, Errol and Oscar gathered as many as they could carry, then ran back to the fence. Errol and Oscar jumped over. Albie crouched to pick up the final ball. They'd done it!

Then he felt something tap him on the shoulder.

Chapter Six

Albie got up slowly and turned round.

An old man stood there. He was leaning on a stick and scowling fiercely.

"I've been watching you," said the man.

It was him! Mr Creaky,
the ghostly-wizarding-spy!
He was even scarier than Albie
had imagined. Albie dropped
the ball and ran.

Albie leaped over the fence and sprinted straight into his dad.

"Hey! What's going on?" Dad yelled.

Mr Creaky's head appeared over the fence.

"I've been watching you," he said again.

Albie, Errol and Oscar hid behind Dad.

"You're a very good footballer,"
Mr Creaky said. He smiled. It
would've been a nice smile if he'd
had any teeth. "Although you need
to practise with your other foot too."

Albie stopped hiding. What did
this old man know about football?

He looked at Dad, who was suddenly pointing at the old man, and smiling a huge smile of his own.

"I know you! It's Billy Mclaren, isn't it? You played for the Tigers when I was a boy. You used to score forty goals a season. You were my hero!"

"But he can't be," said Albie.
"He's a ghost."

"Or a jewel thief," said Errol.

"Or a spy," said Oscar.

"I've been called many things in
my time, but I'll settle for Billy," Mr
Creaky said.

Dad looked so happy Albie
thought he might cry. "Come round
and have a cup of tea."

"I can do better than that," said Billy. "Why don't we sort out my garden? If we knock the fence down you'll have a pitch that's twice as big!"

Albie's face lit up. Imagine that!
A HUGE pitch, a professional
player to coach him and no more
GARDEN OF DOOM!

It was perfect. Just like football.